For Katie and Lucy
C.A.

This edition is
published and distributed
exclusively by
DISCOVERY TOYS
Pleasant Hill, CA

Originally published by
Walker Books Ltd
London

Printed in Italy

First American Edition

ISBN 0-939979-12-8

I Bought My Love a Tabby Cat

Written by Colin West
Illustrated by Caroline Anstey

DISCOVERY TOYS

I bought my love a tabby cat,

A tabby cat, a tabby cat,

My love made him a velvet hat

To wear when we were wed.

I bought my love a billy goat,

A billy goat, a billy goat,

My love made him a woolen coat

To wear when we were wed.

I bought my love a big fat pig,

A big fat pig, a big fat pig,

My love made him a fancy wig

To wear when we were wed.

I bought my love an old gray goose,

An old gray goose, an old gray goose,

My love made him some dainty shoes

To wear when we were wed.

I bought my love a little mule,

A little mule, a little mule,

My love made him a silken shawl

To wear when we were wed.

I bought my love a talking crow,

A talking crow, a talking crow,

My love made him a handsome bow

To wear when we were wed.

And on the day that we were wed,

That we were wed, that we were wed,

I turned to my true love and said,

"Oh, what a sight to see...

"A tabby cat who wears a hat,

"A billy goat who wears a coat,

"A big fat pig who wears a wig,

"An old gray goose who wears new shoes,

"A little mule who wears a shawl,

"A talking crow who wears a bow,

"Oh, heaven help us, who's to say,

Oh, who's to say, oh, who's to say,

Who is the finest dressed today,

'Tis anyone but me."

But since that day when we were wed,

When we were wed, when we were wed,

My love makes clothes for me instead,

As pretty as can be!